POMODORO PENGUIN VISITs ITALY

The Adventures of Pomodoro Penguin, No. 3

by Bryce Westervelt

OPERA GOBBLER BOOKS™

Copyright © 2014 by Bryce Westervelt
Published by Opera Gobbler Books, Centereach, New York

Library of Congress Control Number: 2013922997

ISBN   978-1-941047-04-0 (pb)
            978-1-941047-11-8 (mobi)
            978-1-941047-12-5 (epub)

Layout and interior design by Bryce Westervelt

Please send inquiries, correspondence, and fan mail to:
Pomodoro Penguin
c/o Opera Gobbler Books
PO Box 1376
Selden, NY 11784

www.PomodoroPenguin.com

Printed in the United States of America

First printing: March 2014

To Jenna who, once upon a time, witnessed the "birth" of the Opera Gobbler.

Luciano "Opera Gobbler" Pavoturkey's music (written in italics) can be sung to the tune of *La donna è mobile* from Giuseppe Verdi's opera Rigoletto.

The Italian words *amici miei* mean "my friends"

Early one morning,
two friends out to play,
the penguin and owl
scrambled down the walkway.

Pomodoro exclaimed,
"We're going to be late!
We're supposed to meet Falstaff
by the creek, before eight!"

The two birds came "running"
up to the giraffe.
The big guy looked down
and started to laugh:

"Helloooo little penguin!
You and Violet – you're here!
Let's play with the globe –
our geography sphere!"

"So, let's get started.
I have a suggestion.
Why don't you ask
this here globe the first question?"

With the globe in his hand,
Pomo leaned in to speak.
He shut his eyes tight
and he let out a squeak:

"Magic Globe, Wondrous Globe
this might seem hum-drum,
but where in the world
does pasta come from?"

The globe sprang to life
with a whiz and a bang.
It then spun around
and spoke to the gang:

"This question you ask
is quite a big deal!
You want to know details
of your favorite meal."

"While there's no clear answer
for your brilliant question,
there's one place on Earth
that claims pasta perfection."

"So quick, close your eyes
and count one... two... three...
Then you'll arrive
where your answer will be!"

One.... Two.... Three....

"Hoot, Hootie, Hooo,"
Violet opened her eyes.
"What is this place? Where's the creek?
Hey, you guys!"

"Are you two okay?
Do you know where we are?
This place sure seems odd.
It's really bizarre!"

The trio had landed
on the ground, near a curtain.
Through the drape came a noise –
what it was they weren't certain.

"What is that noise?"
exclaimed the red bird.
"It's the most awesome sound
that I've ever heard."

"Tra la la, gobble dee-
A singing tur-a-key.
I gobble loud and high.
My voice soars through the sky!

Tra la la, gobble doe-
Fans in the front-a-row
and in the balcony,
they all shout "Bra-ah-vo!""

"That guy's amazing,
His voice is so strong.
That singing turkey
can belt out a song."

Pomodoro then wondered,
"Why'd the globe send us here?
I don't see pasta.
Was my question not clear?"

Just then, the turkey
walked back toward the curtain.
He noticed the trio
was looking uncertain.

*"Tra la la, gobble-doe –
I'm Luciano.
You must want autographs
after my sold-out show!"*

"Not quite Mr. Turkey.
Can you please help us, sir?
Where are we? Who are you?
This whole thing's a blur!"

"You are in Italy.
I'm surprised you don't know.
Why else would you show up
backstage at my show?

My name's Luciano –
I'm a real opera star.
My fans flock to hear me
from near and afar."

"You sound like a bird
who can solve our dilemma.
Your voice, as they say,
It is quite a "gem-ah!"

Pomodoro continued,
"We are here on a mission.
Where's the best pasta –
by your definition?"

"You're in the right place
for our pasta is tops!
I'll show you a bunch
of my favorite stops."

"Vermicelli in Venice –
a city afloat.
There, you can eat it
while riding a boat."

"Let's go there," said Pomo,
"if that's the best place.
It's clear to me why
you're assigned to our case!"

"Ravioli in Rome
is eaten outside –
by the old Colosseum –
a real source of pride."

"Alright then," said Violet.
"If this news is true,
then just like the Romans –
we'll do as they do!"

"Farfalle in Florence,
like small butterflies,
though some people claim
that they look like bow ties."

"Ah, cute little butterflies–
they sound really pretty.
Why are we waiting?
That seems like our city!"

"Then there's Milano –
a fashionable place.
Get three-colored Fusilli
stuffed in your face!"

"Bright spiraled pasta?
That seems really fancy!
My stomach is grumbling –
it's sure getting antsy!"

"Penne in Pisa,
by the tower that leans,
is a favorite dish
for grand kings and their queens."

"That tower looks like
it's about to fall down.
We should eat quickly –
and then get out of town!"

"In Naples they serve you
a fine capellini -
like little thin hairs
that are quite teenie-weenie."

"I'll take a big plate,"
exclaimed Pomodoro.
"Let's go there today -
and not wait for tomorrow."

"Verona's a city
that's chock-full of love.
Their ziti's the best –
it's the kind you dream of."

"I want some," said Falstaff.
"Why don't we go there?
That ziti sounds better
Than plain angel hair."

"Vesuvius erupts
with volcanic flavor.
Its cheese manicotti
is something to savor."

"That sounds like the place,"
said the penguin of red.
"Instead of Verona –
let's go there instead."

"Well, Luciano
I just have to ask.
How do you choose?
It's a difficult task.

How do you pick
from all of these dinners?
Italy's pasta –
they all seem like winners!"

"Amici miei –
want to hear something cool?
We Italians, of course,
keep just one simple rule."

The trio leaned close.
Will the turkey come clean?
Which pasta is best
in Italian cuisine?

"As you search the whole world
from end to end.
The best is the pasta
you eat with your friends."

That was the truth
that made them all grin.
One thing's for sure –
It's time to dig in!

THE ADVENTURES OF POMODORO PENGUIN

Pomodoro Penguin Makes a Friend

Pomodoro Penguin and the Geography Giraffe

Pomodoro Penguin Visits Italy

Pomodoro Penguin: Penguins, Penguins All Around

Coming soon:

Pomodoro Penguin and the Library Lemur

Pomodoro Penguin Visits Antarctica

POMODORO PENGUIN HOLIDAY EDITIONS

*Pomodoro Penguin
and the
Halloween Costume Conundrum*

Coming Soon:

*Pomodoro Penguin
and the
Thanksgiving Dinner Dilemma*

PSIA information can be obtained at www.ICGtesting.com
inted in the USA
/OW11s1201300314

9152BV00006B/8/P